PUFFIN BOOKS

YOU CAN'T SAY I'M CRAZY

Robert Swindells left school at the age of fifteen and later joined the Royal Air Force. After his discharge he worked at a variety of jobs, before training and working as a teacher. He is now a full-time writer and lives with his wife Brenda on the Yorkshire Moors. He has written many books for young people, and in 1984 was the winner of The Children's Book Award and The Other Award for his novel *Brother in the Land*. He won the Children's Book Award for a second time in 1990 with *Room 13*.

Robert Swindells

You Can't Say
I'm Crazy

Illustrated by Tony Ross

PUFFIN BOOKS

PUFFIN BOOKS

Published by the Penguin Group
Penguin Books Ltd, 27 Wrights Lane, London W8 5TZ, England
Penguin Books USA Inc., 375 Hudson Street, New York, New York 10014, USA
Penguin Books Australia Ltd, Ringwood, Victoria, Australia
Penguin Books Canada Ltd, 10 Alcorn Avenue, Toronto, Ontario, Canada M4V 3B2
Penguin Books (NZ) Ltd, 182–190 Wairau Road, Auckland 10, New Zealand

Penguin Books Ltd, Registered Offices: Harmondsworth, Middlesex, England

First published by Hamish Hamiliton Ltd 1992
Published in Puffin Books 1994
1 3 5 7 9 10 8 6 4 2

The moral right of the author and illustrator has been asserted

Printed in England by Clays Ltd, St Ives plc
Filmset in Baskerville

Gaz and the Guy Fawkes Plot

Chapter 1

"I BET THIS is the best gang hut in the world," said Gaz, peering out at the drizzle which fell relentlessly on Sophie's dad's allotment. "You've got an ace dad, Sophie."

Sophie grinned. "I know, and I take after him. You're the boss Gaz, but I'm the brains."

"And I'm the muscles," said Jim. "Pip can be the fat."

"Thanks a bunch," growled Pip, stuffing a fistful of rags up the sleeve of the old jacket he was working on. "What time did you say the

competition was, Gaz?"

"Two o'clock."

"We'd better get a move on then, hadn't we?"

"Why?" Gaz looked at his watch. "It's not even twelve yet. Plenty of time."

It was Saturday, November the fifth. Bonfire night. There was to be a giant bonfire on the school playing field. It would be lit at seven o'clock but before that, in the afternoon, Mr Roper the P.E. teacher was judging a Guy Fawkes competition. The prize for the best guy was a radio cassette player, and Gaz wanted it for the hut. They already had four folding chairs, a table, a square of threadbare carpet and some posters. The cassette player would add a finishing touch to the plastic watchman's shelter Sophie's

dad had given them, turning it into a really posh headquarters.

"You know what the hardest part is, don't you?" said Jim.

"No." Sophie shook her head. "What is the hardest part?"

"The face. Think about the best guys you've ever seen. They've got brilliant clothes and they're stuffed really full so they sit up like real people instead of flopping about. They've even got hats and gloves and shoes. But the faces always spoil them. Dead white they are, with eyes and mouths and noses done in felt tip or make-up or something, and no hair. They sit there with stupid fixed expressions, like Pip when Miss Cawley asks him something. It ruins the whole effect."

Pip threw a handful of rags at Jim, and Gaz said, "So what brilliant

5

idea have you got for a face, Jim?"

Jim shrugged. "I haven't. I thought I'd mention it, that's all."

"Cretin." Gaz looked at Sophie. "What about you, brains? Have you got any ideas?"

Sophie frowned. "I suppose we could cut a face out of a magazine – one of those big coloured ones from a toothpaste ad or something – and stick it on. It'd look better than felt tip anyway."

"Hey, yes!" Jim's eyes shone. "That's a really sound idea, Gaz."

"I know," said Gaz. "I'm glad I thought of it. Anybody know where there's a magazine?"

They'd brought packed lunches so they wouldn't have to go home, and by one o'clock the Guy Fawkes was done. It wore an ancient suit Pip's uncle had

6

given them, some wellies that Gaz had grown out of, a wide-brimmed hat from Jim's mum and a pair of worn-out driving gloves. They'd found a plastic carrier full of magazines by somebody's dustbin and emptied it on the floor of the hut, rummaging through till they found a suitable picture to stick over the blank, white face. Now it sat bolt upright in Sophie's little sister's old pram with a brilliant smile on its tanned, handsome features. The gang looked at it.

"D'you think it's anything like the real Guy Fawkes?" asked Pip.

"Oh, sure," laughed Jim. "He did a lot of sunbathing and brushed his teeth ten times a day and never went anywhere without his pink wedding hat. It's a well-known fact."

"Well, anyway, I think he looks great," defended Sophie.

Gaz nodded. "So do I. That cassette player's as good as ours already."

Chapter 2

AT HALF PAST one they pushed the
pram out of the hut and began
wheeling it through the village. The
drizzle had stopped. Haxley was a
quiet place, especially on a Saturday
lunchtime, and there weren't many
people about. Gaz and the others had
hoped to cadge a bit of firework money
by saying 'penny for the guy' to every
adult they met, but they hardly met
any, and those they did meet had been
stopped by other kids and were
reluctant to fork out yet again. One or
two fished small coins out of their

pockets, but most simply muttered something the kids didn't catch and walked on. When they reached the end of the village they'd collected the fantastic sum of seven pence.

"Great," growled Gaz. "We can buy a sparkler and take turns holding it."

"We've got one more chance," said Pip. "Look – old Wurzel's at his gate."

They were approaching the last house in the village – a ramshackle, tumbledown cottage with a tin roof and a jungle of a garden where Wurzel lived alone. He wasn't really called Wurzel. Nobody knew his real name because he'd come to Haxley from somewhere else and hardly ever spoke to anyone. His clothes were so scruffy that the villagers had christened him Wurzel after a scarecrow on the telly. You'd see him now and then in the village shop or shuffling along the lane with his head down, but mostly he stayed indoors. Now he was standing at his peeling, blistered gate with the jungle at his back and a battered trilby on his head.

Jim gave Gaz a push. "Go on – ask him."

"You," said Gaz. He was a bit wary of old Wurzel.

"No, you. You're the boss of this gang."

"He might grab me."

"Will he heck. He's harmless, my dad says."

"Well, go fetch your dad then," Gaz retorted. "And he can ask."

'I'll ask," volunteered Sophie. "I don't mind."

Gaz looked at her. "Go on then."

They drew level with the gate.

Wurzel was bending down with his back to them, doing something to a clump of weeds.

"Penny for the guy!" cried Sophie, clinking the seven pence in her hand.

The old man straightened slowly and turned. "Are you addressing me, young woman?"

To the gang's surprise, his voice sounded quite posh. Sophie grinned, nodding. "Yes. I said, 'Penny for the guy.'"

"Hmm." Wurzel leaned over the gate and peered shortsightedly at the guy. "Guy Fawkes in effigy, eh?"

"No," said Jim. "In a pram."

"Don't be impertinent, boy." Wurzel glared at Jim, who took a couple of quick steps backwards. "I haven't got a penny for you, but I can help you win the competition."

"The competition?" Gaz was amazed the old man knew about it. "That'd be great, Mister Wur – I mean, thanks a lot, Mister – er . . ."

"Wurzel will do," said Wurzel. "It's as good a name as any. Wait here a moment."

The gang stood, red-faced and open-mouthed as the old man turned and pushed his way into the tangle of weeds and shrubs gone wild.

"He knows," croaked Pip. "He knows we call him Wurzel."

Sophie nodded. "He doesn't seem to mind."

"Told you he was harmless, didn't I?" crowed Jim.

"You backed off pretty quick when he told you off though," said Gaz. "Wonder what he's gone for?"

They weren't left wondering long.

There was a swishing, crackling noise
and Wurzel reappeared, carrying
something in both hands.

"Here." He held it out and the
children saw that it was a mask,
complete with a hat and some long,
dark hair.

"Put that on," said the old man,
"and you'll have the finest guy
anybody ever saw."

It was true. When Gaz had fitted the
mask over the guy's head you'd have
thought Guy Fawkes himself was
sitting in that pram. The face was so

17

lifelike under the conical hat it seemed
to move, and the hair fell over the
effigy's shoulders in a most convincing
way.

"Hey!" gasped Pip. "It's dead
realistic, Gaz."

Gaz nodded. "I know." He looked

at the old man. "Thanks, Mister.
Thanks a lot. I mean it."

Wurzel nodded. "I know you do.
And now you'd better be getting along
or you'll miss the competition."

They thanked him again and walked
on, feeling the prize within their grasp.

Chapter 3

WHEN GAZ AND the gang reached the school playing field, they found that most of the others had arrived before them. Kids were scurrying back and forth, dragging old furniture or carrying armfuls of branches and assorted rubbish, building the bonfire under Mr Roper's watchful eye. A line of prams and home-made carts stood along one edge of the playground, and the guys in them seemed to be watching the pile grow higher.

Gaz did a quick count. "Wow!" he gasped. "Twenty-one guys."

Sophie nodded. "None like ours though. They might as well go home for all the chance they've got."

They parked their pram in the line and went to help with the bonfire. There was tons of stuff, and it was twenty past two before they had it all piled up. With everything on, the heap was six metres high. Everybody stood admiring it, taking a breather.

After a while Mr Roper said, "Right. Competition time. The winning team gets the prize, and their guy goes on top of the heap with bangers in its pockets. The others will be propped on the lower slopes where the flames will reach them sooner. Stand by your guys."

The kids went and stood beside their entries and the teacher walked slowly along the line, inspecting the effigies.

When he came to the gang's guy, he
stopped.

"How on earth did you make that
head?" he cried.

Gaz shrugged. "We just fitted some
bits and pieces together, sir, and this is
how it came out."

"Bits and pieces." Mr Roper shook
his head in disbelief. "It's magnificent,
Gary. No other word for it."

It was no contest. When the judging

was over, Gaz went up and accepted the prize and everybody clapped. They crowded round the old pram to gaze at the fabulous guy, pinching and poking to see what it was made of.

"It's like a real person," said Mandy Wright. "It'll be a shame to burn it."

Mr Roper called everybody together. "Right, listen. I'm staying in school to keep an eye on things. You go home, get some tea and be back here at six-thirty wearing something warm. We put the guys on the heap at half past six, fireworks start at a quarter to seven and we light the bonfire at seven. Any questions?"

There were none. The kids began to disperse. Gaz capered across the playground holding his prize aloft like the FA Cup while Sophie, Pip and Jim danced round him singing, "We won, cha-cha-cha," and the teacher called after them, "Well done, you four."

"Well done, Wurzel," murmured Sophie.

Nobody heard her.

Chapter 4

THEY MET AT a quarter past six in the hut. Gaz had brought the cassette player. They stood it on the table and looked at it.

"Has it got batteries?" asked Jim.

Gaz nodded.

"Let's try it out then," suggested Pip.

They played part of a tape, then locked up the hut and hurried along to the field. It was just after half-past when they got there. All the kids were waiting.

"Ah, at last," said Mr Roper.

"Trying out your prize, were you?"

Gaz grinned. "How'd you guess, sir?"

The teacher smiled. "It wasn't hard. Fetch the winning entry, then."

They wheeled the guy towards the bonfire heap. The other kids followed with theirs. Mr Roper propped a short ladder against the heap and was about to lift the winning guy out of its pram when something amazing happened. As the teacher reached for the effigy it jerked itself away from his hands, scrambled out of the pram and ran off across the field, losing its hat in the process. The kids gasped in amazement as the guy squeezed through a hole in the fence and ran off into the darkness.

Mr Roper gazed after it, open-mouthed. He shook his head and

knuckled his eyes as though there
might be something wrong with his
vision. Then he turned to Gaz.

"Who was that?" he demanded.

"Er – nobody, sir. It was just a guy,
sir."

"Rubbish, lad. You dressed
somebody up, didn't you?"

"No sir, honestly. Ask the others,
sir."

The teacher was adamant. "You
dressed somebody up. You must
have."

"No sir," cried Sophie. "It was here
all afternoon, sitting in the pram. You
saw it, sir. It never moved. A real
person couldn't . . ."

"Now that's enough, Sophie, d'you
hear?" Mr Roper didn't often shout,
but he was shouting now.

As Gaz and the gang gaped at one

another in disbelief, he said, "We don't like cheats at Haxley Junior, Gary. First thing Monday morning I want that cassette player on my desk so that it can be presented to Mandy Wright, whose guy came second."

"But sir . . ." croaked Gaz.

The kids were giving them dirty looks. There was some hissing and booing.

"Never mind 'But sir'," snapped the teacher. "You dressed up a real person and pretended it was a guy. No wonder it looked realistic."

"But sir, we didn't. We made the guy sir, and old Wurzel gave us . . ."

"Nonsense, Gary. You and your friends can stay if you want to, but I expect to find that prize on my desk at ten to nine on Monday morning." He turned to Mandy Wright. "Bring your

33

guy over here, Mandy."

The four friends stayed to watch the fireworks, but they didn't enjoy them. Nobody would speak to them, or even stand nearby.

Soon after Mr Roper lit the fire Sophie said, "This is awful, Gaz. I'm off home."

Pip nodded. "Me too."

Gaz looked at Jim. "How about you?"

Jim shrugged. "Not much fun, is it?"

"Okay then," growled Gaz. "We'll go, but everybody'll think we really did cheat, you know."

"They do now," said Sophie.

They went back to the hut. It was stil the best gang hut in the world, but they couldn't enjoy it now. They sat, gazing out into the darkness.

"How the heck did it happen?" asked Pip.

Gaz shrugged. "Dunno. I wouldn't have believed it if I hadn't seen it."

Jim shook his head. "Me neither."

"I know it sounds daft," murmured Sophie, "but I think it was magic."

"Magic?" Gaz looked at her. "There's no such thing as magic, Sophie. No. Someone must have swiped our guy and put a kid in its

place. Someone who didn't want us to win."

"How could they?" cried Sophie scornfully. "Mr Roper was there all the time. It was magic I tell you, and the magic was in Wurzel's mask."

Gaz shook his head. "I dunno about that, Sophie, but I know one thing. It's not fair. We've done nothing wrong, but we lose our prize and everybody thinks we cheated."

"Yeah," moaned Jim. "Rotten, isn't it?"

They sat, grumbling and moaning till it was time to split up and go home. They hadn't played any tapes, and when they left the hut, Gaz took the player with him.

Chapter 5

THEY DIDN'T MEET next day. They were
too fed up, and it was a gloomy
foursome which met outside Jim's
house on Monday morning for the
walk to school. Gaz had the cassette
player with him, in its original box.
They mumbled greetings to one
another and dawdled through the
village even more slowly than usual.

"I feel like wagging off," said Pip.

Jim nodded. "So do I. Shall we?"

Gaz shook his head. "We'd only get
into worse trouble. We know we didn't
cheat, even if nobody else does. We'll

just have to stick together and put up with it."

"I wish we could prove it though," said Sophie. "D'you think old Wurzel'd put in a word for us? I know you think I'm daft, but I'm sure it was his mask which made the guy come alive."

Gaz shook his head again. "No chance. He doesn't like people. He wouldn't come within a mile of school."

They walked on, ignored by all the other kids.

The school gate was in sight when Mr Roper's yellow mini passed them, signalling right. They followed it with their eyes, waiting for the teacher to sound his horn as he always did to scatter the knot of kids hanging round the gate. As the car approached the

gateway, a boy burst out of the hedge and ran straight out in front of it. There was a screech of brakes as the driver tried to stop, but he didn't have a chance. Fifty kids gazed in horror as the mini struck the boy, hurling him into the ditch where he lay crumpled with one leg sticking out at an impossible angle.

"Come on!" cried Sophie. "We've got to help him."

She ran towards the fallen boy and
the others followed. Kids were
converging on the scene from all
directions. Mr Roper had leapt from
his car and was running back. Sophie
got there first, going down on one knee
beside the motionless figure. She
reached out to brush hair from the face
and cried out as the victim's features
were revealed.

Mr Roper arrived, fighting his way through a throng of kids.

"Who is it, Sophie?" he gasped. "Is he badly hurt?"

Sophie looked up, shaking her head. "It's not a kid at all, sir. It's our guy – the one that ran away."

"Let me see."

The babble of voices increased in volume as kids at the front, who could see the effigy, relayed the news to those pressing in from behind. The teacher knelt, plucking and prodding at the guy, thankful yet deeply puzzled to find no blood, no bone. He pulled off the mask, and underneath was a cut-out paper face with perfect teeth.

"Hey Gaz," said a voice in the crush. "How'd you make it move?"

Gaz, who had pushed and shoved his way to the front, shook his head. "I

didn't. I don't know anything about it."

His mind was in a whirl. He felt relieved: relieved that nobody was hurt, and that this had happened before witnesses so that everybody could see he hadn't cheated, but he was frightened too. He'd laughed at Sophie's mention of magic but it seemed she was right, and Gaz found this really scary. He'd have preferred to go on believing that somebody had switched their guy for a real person.

The ashpile on the playing field was still glowing, and some of the kids fed it with rocket sticks and the cases of spent fireworks till they had a bit of a blaze going. Gaz could tell by the way they worked that he wasn't the only one feeling scared. He knew what the fire was for; knew what they wanted him to do. When he threw the guy into the flames there was a noise from the onlookers like a sigh, and nobody moved till it was all burned up. It was over by the time the bell went, and everybody felt better. When Gaz took the cassette player to Mr Roper, the teacher told him he might keep it, but Gaz had a talk with the gang and they decided to give it to Mandy Wright.

They hadn't cheated – not on purpose – but they'd certainly had help from Wurzel, which wasn't really fair.

They didn't burn the mask. They tried to return it, Monday teatime, on the way home. They screwed up their courage and waded through the

undergrowth up to the old man's door but he wouldn't open it. They knocked and called but Wurzel pretended he wasn't in, so Gaz hung the mask on the doorknob and they left it there. None of them spoke as they strolled away, but they knew they'd never walk through Wurzel's gate again.

There are more ways than one of getting a cassette player, and they got one the following spring. They'd spent the winter washing cars, tidying gardens and clearing snow from people's driveways, and by the end of March they'd earned the cash they needed. There was no magic involved so it wasn't quick or easy but it wasn't scary either, and because they'd worked hard to get it, they felt the player was really theirs.

"Magic's all right in stories," said

Gaz, "but it's dodgy stuff to get mixed up in."

Sophie smiled. "I know a teacher who'd probably agree with you," she said.

Gaz and the Otherworld Tree

Chapter 1

A SATURDAY MORNING in April. Gaz, Pip and Sophie were sitting in the hut, waiting for Jim. It was warm and sunny and they'd planned to be in Haxley Woods by this time. Gaz looked at his watch.

"Twenty past nine," he grumbled. "And we told him nine o'clock. What's he playing at?"

"He's probably having to look after Timothy while his mum goes shopping," said Sophie. "Little brothers can be a real drag, you know."

"Big ones are worse," put in Pip. "Our Chris beats me up and pinches my stuff all the time."

Sophie nodded. "It's all right for you, Gaz. It must be great being the only one. I bet you're really spoilt."

"No, I'm not!" Gaz retorted. "I wish I had brothers and sisters, I can tell you. It's rotten being by yourself."

Pip was about to argue when the allotment gate clicked and Jim stuck his head round the door.

"Sorry I'm late," he said. "I had to mind our Tim while Mum went down the shops."

"Told you," crowed Sophie.

"Told 'em what?" Jim asked.

"Oh, we were talking about sisters and brothers," said Sophie.

Jim pulled a face. "You can keep 'em," he growled.

It was good in the woods. Buds were bursting. Birds were building. The sun warmed the earth and tender shoots came poking through to get their share of it. There were celandines and hazel catkins and a fresh, soily smell.

"Let's play tag," suggested Pip. "You're it, Gaz."

Gaz didn't want to be it, but the others scattered before he had time to argue, and he had to decide who to chase. He went after Sophie, but she easily outran him on her long, thin legs. He gave up and ran after Pip, determined to touch him so he'd be it. Pip wasn't a bad runner, but Gaz kept after him and tagged him when he stumbled over a root. Pip immediately chased Gaz, but Gaz dodged round a holly bush and Pip took off after Jim.

Gaz stood by the holly bush, getting

his breath back. He hadn't been in this bit of the wood before. He looked around and saw a very old oak with a hole at the foot of its trunk. He grinned. A hollow tree, fat enough to stand up in by the look of it. He could crawl in there and they'd never find him. It was against the rules of course. You weren't supposed to hide, because if you did it wasn't tag any more, it was hide and seek, but he didn't care. It would be a good laugh.

He got down on his hands and knees, crawled inside the tree and stood up. There was plenty of room, and there was something else as well. High up in the other side of the trunk was a second hole, like a sort of window. It was smaller than the one he'd crawled in through, and it was above his head, but Gaz reckoned he'd

be able to escape through it if
somebody found his hiding place. He
sat down. The two holes let in plenty
of daylight so it wasn't even spooky.

He waited. Now and then he heard
his friends calling to one another but
they sounded a long way off, and after
a while he didn't hear them any more.
He looked at his watch and saw that

he'd been there twenty-five minutes. It was a bit chilly inside the oak and he was beginning to ache from sitting scrunched up. He stood up, but that didn't make him any warmer.

"I might as well forget it," he told himself. "Nobody's going to come. They've probably gone home." He was about to get down and crawl out when he had an idea. "I know," he whispered. "I'll get out through the window."

He did. It wasn't easy scrambling up the inside of the tree trunk and he had to wriggle a bit to get through the hole, but he made it. He dropped onto the grass and stood for a moment, listening. Wind in the trees and a twittering of birds, but no voices. He started walking, looking back a few times to remember where the hollow tree was so he could show the others tomorrow.

It was half past eleven when he got home. The house was empty. He looked through the kitchen window and saw his mum in the back garden, pegging out clothes. Somebody was moving about upstairs, so that's where his dad must be.

Chapter 2

HE DIDN'T KNOW why, but somehow
things didn't feel quite right. He
glanced round the kitchen. That
biscuit tin on top of the fridge. That
wasn't there this morning, was it?
They didn't have a biscuit tin like that.
He shrugged. Mum must have bought
it while he was out. Or Dad. And that
was another thing. Dad. On a day like
this – a dry, warm Saturday – you'd
expect to find him in the garden. He
was mad on gardening, Gaz's dad, but
nothing was happening out there
today, except . . .

Washing. But Mum never washed on a Saturday. Monday was washday. Saturdays she went down the supermarket, then read a book in her room or in the garden while Dad watched sport on telly. Gaz looked out of the window again. His mum had nearly finished. The line was almost full, the blue plastic basket nearly empty. Blue? He could've sworn his mum's clothes-basket was yellow. She must have bought a new one along with the biscuit tin.

But hang on a minute – look at that washing. All those jeans. Whose are those? He counted. Five pairs. One's mine, and that one there's Dad's, but where have the rest come from? Surely Mum wouldn't have gone out and bought three pairs of jeans and washed them, brand new? What's going on?

He crossed the kitchen and walked along the hallway to the living room. He was feeling really nervous by now. It was as though someone had come along while he was out and made lots of little changes to his home. Perhaps they had. Maybe it was Mum and Dad playing a trick on him. Or perhaps, he thought, everything's the same and it's me who's gone nutty.

The living room was all right. Neat and tidy, nothing out of place. Just as Mum liked it. He stood in the doorway, looking at it. Feeling better. Everything was the same in here. Nothing missing, nothing new. He smiled. So his mum had been out and bought a few things and Dad wasn't doing the garden. So what? He turned and crossed the hallway to the stairs. He wasn't going nutty, and nobody

was playing tricks. He'd lie on his bed
and listen to some tapes till it was time
to eat.

He was halfway up when a voice
called, "That you, Gary?"

A girl's voice, coming from the spare

room. He stopped, his mind racing. A girl? What girl? Cousin Rachel? She was the only girl who ever came here, but she lived a hundred miles away in Leicester and besides, if she was here, where were Auntie Pam and Uncle Kev?

He swallowed and called out, "Yes, it's me. Who's that?"

"Who d'you think, thickhead?" said the voice, scornfully. "You've been in my cassettes again, haven't you?"

Cassettes? What cassettes? The only cassettes in this house were his. In this house . . .

"Oh, no!" He glanced about him, wildly. "The wrong house. I must have come to the wrong house. I'm halfway up the stairs in somebody else's house. They'll think I'm a burglar or something."

He turned, and was about to rush downstairs when he heard footsteps in the hallway and his mother looked up at him.

Chapter 3

"GARY," SHE SAID, "where have you put the fish and chips?"

"Fish and chips?" He stared at her. It couldn't be the wrong house if Mum was here, could it? But what was she on about?

"Yes, fish and chips. Don't tell me you've forgotten to fetch them, Gary?"

"I – I didn't know I was supposed to fetch them, Mum."

"Of course you were supposed to fetch them. Why d'you think I gave you four pounds and a plastic carrier? Kevin and your dad'll be here in a

minute wanting their dinner. They'll be in a rush because they're off to the match. You'd better run to that chippy, and sharp about it if you know what's good for you."

"But I – you didn't give me four pounds, Mum. I've been up the woods with Jim and Pip and Sophie. I just got back."

His mother opened her mouth, but before she could say anything a plump girl of about twelve came out of the spare room and looked over the bannister. "Mum, tell him. He's been messing around with my cassettes again."

His mother frowned at him. "How many times must I tell you to leave your sister's things alone, Gary? That room's Donna's and you're to stay out of it."

70

"Sister?" Gaz gaped up at the girl. "I've never seen her before, Mum. I don't know anybody called Donna. What's happening to me?"

His mother made fists of her hands and rested them on her hips. She looked extremely angry.

"Gary Parsons, I don't know what sort of game you're playing, but it's going to stop right now. Come down off those stairs, find that money, and get along to the fish shop. You know what'll happen if you make your brother late for the match."

"Brother? I haven't got a br . . ."

Before Gaz could finish, the front door opened and a boy walked in carrying something wrapped in newspaper.

"Here y'are, Mum!" he chirped. "Fish and chips five times, and

there's your change."

Gaz stared at the boy. There was something familiar about him. His mother was staring too.

"Gary," she gasped, "if you're here, who's this boy halfway up my stairs?"

Gaz glanced at the boy and gulped. "It's me!" he croaked. "Or else my double."

He looked around him. The girl called Donna was coming down the stairs. The woman he'd mistaken for his mother was coming up. His double was in the doorway, gaping up at him in disbelief, blocking the way. He was trapped.

Chapter 4

AT THAT MOMENT he heard the back
door open and a man's voice called
out, "Hello love, we're home!"

It sounded just like Dad, but he
knew it wasn't. It was that other kid's
dad. And Donna's. And Kevin's. And
if he didn't get out of here right now he
didn't know what might happen.

"Eric!" the woman cried. "Come
here quick. We've got a . . . oh!"

She gasped, falling back against the
bannister as Gaz charged past her. His
double was still blocking the doorway.
Gaz let out a blood-curdling yell and

ran straight at him. The boy dropped
the parcel which burst open, spilling
chips on the doormat. Gaz barged into
him, knocking him aside, and pelted
down the garden path which looked
exactly like his own. He didn't know
where he was, or where he was going.
He only knew he must avoid capture at
all costs. He swerved right and ran
along the pavement, past familiar
houses and trees and hedges he
thought he knew. He didn't know why,
but he was heading for the woods.
Maybe that hollow tree had something
to do with all this weird stuff that was
happening to him. If not, at least he
could hide in it till his pursuers gave
up.

He was panting by the time he
reached the woods. He couldn't hear
anyone behind him. Perhaps they'd

given up the chase, but he daren't glance round to see. He kept running till he saw the hollow oak ahead. When he reached it he turned. There was nobody in sight.

"Thank goodness!" he gasped. "I couldn't have run much further."

He leaned against the tree getting his breath back, feeling the rough bark through his jacket. After a minute he turned and looked up at the hole in the trunk.

Everything was okay, he thought, till I crawled out of this tree. Since then, either the world's gone crazy or I have. The notion that he might be mad scared him badly. Maybe that's it, he thought. Maybe I've always had a sister called Donna and a brother Kevin. Maybe we've always had fish and chips for Saturday lunch and I've

just forgotten. Perhaps I've lost my memory. You hear of people losing their memory. They don't know who they are or where they live.

He was trembling, talking to himself. That's one of the signs, according to Sophie. Talking to yourself. Come on then. Don't hang about. Do something. What, though? I know. Climb the tree. Go back through the hole. Maybe then . . .

He found a handhold and a foothold
and began to climb. He paused once or
twice to glance over his shoulder, but
there was nobody. He had a
tremendous tussle getting into the hole.
In the end he had to wriggle through
head first. All the time he was doing it
he expected to feel somebody's hands
grab his ankles and haul him out
backwards, and when he finally got

inside he had to do some high-level acrobatics to get himself the right way up, but he managed it.

Standing in the half-darkness he hesitated. Suppose he crawled out and everything was still the same? Suppose he got home and found Donna there, and Kevin, and his own double, and a mum and dad who weren't really his? Well, he told himself, you can't spend the rest of your life inside a hollow tree. He got down on his hands and knees, crawled through the hole and stood up.

Everything looked the same. Birds called back and forth. Sunlight glinted through the trees and he smelled the same soily smell. He knew what he had to do now. He had to go home and find out whether everything was as it should be. It was scary, but he had no choice.

He was about to start walking when he heard a voice in the distance.

"Gaz!" it yelled. "Where've you hidden yourself, you rotten cheat?"

Sophie! His heart kicked.

"Here!" he cried. "I'm over here."

He began running towards the voice, which was shouting that they were supposed to be playing tag, not hide and seek. Other voices joined in and after a moment he saw Sophie, Pip and

Jim coming towards him. He ran to
them.

"Where've you been?" demanded
Sophie. "We've been looking all over."

Gaz shook his head. "I don't know
where I've been," he told her, "but
I'm sure happy to be back."

"Yes," Pip complained. "But it's
after twelve, Gaz. We've spent half the

morning looking for you and now we'll have to go straight home."

"I know," said Gaz. "I'm sorry. I got sort of lost, and I do want to go home. I – want to see Mum and Dad." He hesitated a moment, then added, "I want to see if Donna and Kevin are at home."

It was a terrifying moment. What if Pip said, "Of course they're at home. Where d'you think they are – on the moon?"

He didn't. Nobody did. They looked at him strangely and Pip said, "Who the heck are Donna and Kevin, Gaz?"

His heart soared. "Oh," he laughed. "They're nobody. They're just the sister and brother I don't have."

Pip shook his head. "You're crazy, Gaz, d'you know that?"

Gaz laughed out loud. "That's just

where you're wrong," he cried. "I thought I was, but I'm not."

He lifted his arms and began a slow, capering dance, chanting as his body swooped and turned.

> *Call me lazy*
> *Or hazy*
> *Or say I'm a daisy*
> *But one thing you can't say*
> *You can't say I'm crazy.*

They were laughing at him, but Gaz didn't care. He was going home.

Also in Young Puffin

Ricky's Summertime Christmas Present

Frank Rodgers

FOR RICKY BROWN. DO NOT WAIT UNTIL CHRISTMAS. OPEN NOW!

Ricky is puzzled to receive a Christmas present in the middle of summer from an uncle he didn't know he had. But the present leads him on an exciting adventure to rescue his long-lost uncle from danger.

Also in Young Puffin

Willie Whiskers

Margaret Gordon

**"I'm a hero," said Willie Whiskers.
"I'm a hero because I eat too much
and because I'm so fat."**

Willie Whiskers is a very greedy little
mouse – he is as round and fat as a hairy
golf ball. But he doesn't care, even when
he gets squashed in a slipper, tied up in a
hair ribbon, or half drowned in a bowl of
custard. His family think he should be
doing sums instead, but all is forgiven the
day Willie saves them from disaster, just
because he *is* so fat!